# Cinderella

Illustrated by
Gill Guile

Brimax · Newmarket · England

Cinderella lives in a big house with her two ugly sisters.
Her sisters are unkind to her and make her do all the housework.
They make her dust and polish, wash the clothes, do the dishes, and help them get ready when they want to go out.

One day a letter arrives for the ugly sisters. It is an invitation to a ball at the palace!
“Am I invited?” asks Cinderella.
“Of course not!” says one of the sisters. “You have to help us get ready. You can’t go!”
“Besides,” says the other sister, “You don’t have a dress. You only have those rags!”

On the day of the ball, Cinderella helps her sisters get ready. She washes their dresses and polishes their shoes. By the time they have gone, Cinderella is so tired she sits by the fire and sobs. “I wish I could go to the ball!” she cries.

Suddenly she hears a voice.
"Don't worry. You shall go to the ball!"
"Who are you?" asks Cinderella.
She is frightened.
"I am your fairy godmother," says the stranger. "I will get you ready for the ball."

"Bring me a big pumpkin!" says the fairy godmother. She touches it with her wand and turns it into a coach. Next, Cinderella brings her four white mice. The fairy godmother turns them into white horses. She turns three lizards into a coach driver and two footmen. She turns Cinderella's rags into a gown. On Cinderella's feet are a pair of glass slippers.

"Now you are ready to go," says the fairy godmother. "But remember to leave before the clock strikes twelve. At midnight your dress will turn to rags and your coach will turn back into a pumpkin!" Cinderella sets off in the coach to the ball.

When Cinderella arrives at the ball she sees her two sisters. They do not know who she is. Cinderella dances with the Prince all night long. He will not dance with anyone else. Cinderella is very happy. She forgets her fairy godmother's warning about leaving before midnight.

Suddenly the clock strikes twelve! Cinderella runs out of the palace and down the steps. Her dress turns into rags and the coach becomes a pumpkin again. As she runs away, one of her glass slippers falls off. The Prince finds it. He says to a footman, "Find the girl who owns this slipper. I want to marry her."

The footman searches the land for the owner of the slipper. Finally he comes to Cinderella's house. Her sisters try on the glass slipper. It does not fit either of them. Cinderella tries it on. The slipper fits perfectly. The Prince marries Cinderella and they live happily ever after.

# Can you find five differences between these two pictures?